KING BIDGOOD'S IN THE BATHTUB

WRITTEN BY
AUDREY WOOD

ILLUSTRATED BY
DON WOOD

SCHOLASTIC INC.

New York Toronto London Auckland Sydney
Mexico City New Delhi Hong Kong Buenos Aires

ISBN 0-439-63240-4

12 11   9/0

Printed in the U.S.A.   40

First Scholastic paperback printing, March 2004

For Edwin Cook Brewer

"Help! Help!" cried the Page when the sun came up.
"King Bidgood's in the bathtub, and he won't get out!
Oh, who knows what to do?"

"I do!" cried the Knight when the sun came up.
"Get out! It's time to battle!"

"Come in!" cried the King, with a boom, boom, boom.

"Today we battle in the tub!"

"Help! Help!" cried the Page when the sun got hot.
"King Bidgood's in the bathtub, and he won't get out!
Oh, who knows what to do?"

"I do!" cried the Queen when the sun got hot.
"Get out! It's time to lunch!"
"Come in!" cried the King, with a yum, yum, yum.

"Today we lunch in the tub!"

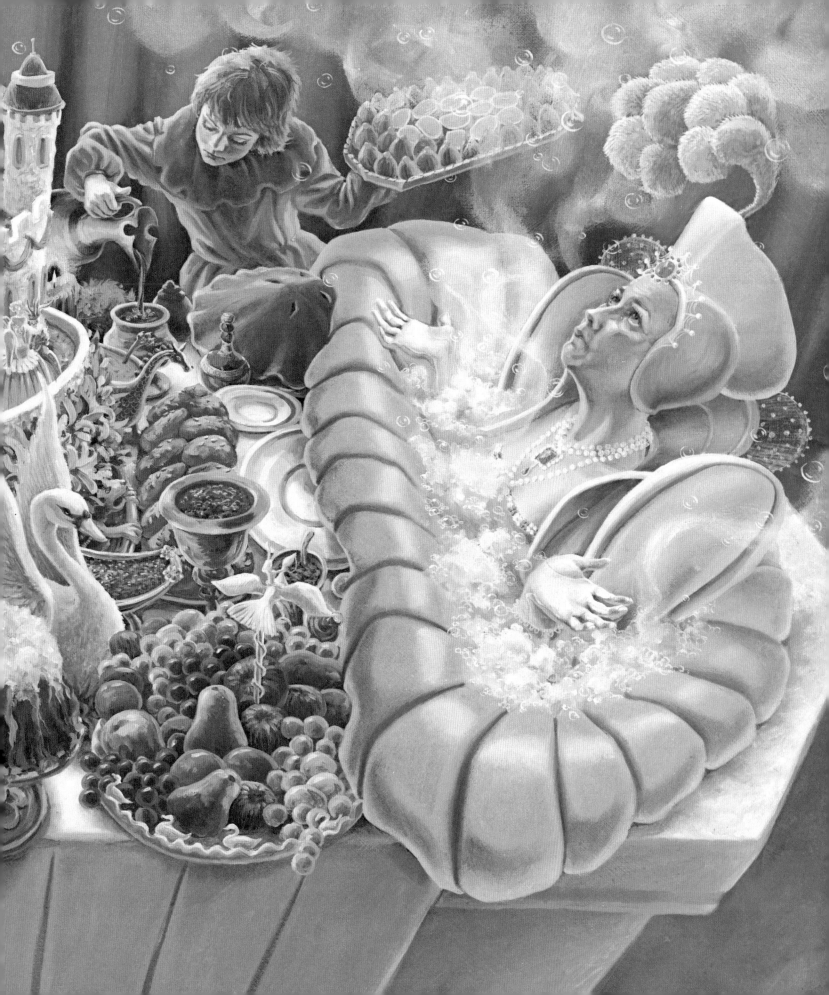

"Help! Help!" cried the Page when the sun sank low.
"King Bidgood's in the bathtub, and he won't get out!
Oh, who knows what to do?"

"I do!" cried the Duke when the sun sank low.
"Get out! It's time to fish!"
"Come in!" cried the King, with a trout, trout, trout.

"Today we fish in the tub!"

"Help! Help!" cried the Page when the night got dark.
"King Bidgood's in the bathtub, and he won't get out!
Oh, who knows what to do?"

"We do!" cried the Court when the night got dark.
"Get out for the Masquerade Ball!"
"Come in!" cried the King, with a jig, jig, jig.

"Tonight we dance in the tub!"

"Help! Help!" cried the Court when the moon shone bright.
"King Bidgood's in the bathtub, and he won't get out!
Oh, who knows what to do?
Who knows what to do?"

"I do!" said the Page when the moon shone bright,
and then he pulled the plug.

Glub, glub, glub!